Dear Reader

The book you are about to read, is a collection of poetry written at various stages in my life. They are dedicated to loved ones of mine and of others who have passed on. I have also added poems that have other meanings to myself and the people who I wrote them for. I believe that I have grown a lot personally since I wrote my first poem and I look forward to continuing.

I gladly share my inner thoughts with you and upon finishing my book, I hope you find at least one poem that moves you in some way or another.

Thank you for your support.

Ray Phoenix

ISBN: 9781089109372

Contents

Aberfan

One word is all it took to send me back in years,

One word is all it took to remember all the tears.

One word is all it took to cause my hands to shake,

One word is all it took to remind me of the heartbreak.

One word is all it took to have me on my knees,

One word is all it took to cause my heart to freeze.

One word is all it took to remind me of that day,

One word is all it took to make me start to pray.

One word is all it took to see what was destroyed,

One word is all it took to make me feel annoyed.

One word is all it took to remember the destruction,

One word is all it took to recall this man-made construction.

One word is all it took to remember who was to blame,

One word is all it took to think of them with shame.

One word is all it took to remind me I was small,

One word is all it took to recall it all.

One word is all took to wish it was a dream,

One word is all it took to recall each scream.

One word is all it took to pray for my fellow man,

One word is all it took and that was Aberfan.

A Mother's Wrath

In a place where we aren't free,

They took my children away from me.

Tying me up as they stripped me bare,

Cutting away my beautiful hair.

Leaving me alone to dehydrate,

As for my death they gladly wait.

Tightening ropes until I bleed,

Calling it just a political need.

Though in such pain I will not shout,

For I'll escape there is no doubt.

Slowly the ropes loosen their grip,

And from them one night I quietly slip.

Stealing their clothes, I quickly dress,

Pointing the gun, I steadily press.

There is no sound for it is silent,

It is there fault I became so violent.

They should have known that I would fight,

As they took my children far out of sight.

Loaded with weapons I destroy the place,

A mother's wrath they now must face.

A New Ma

Today I'm getting myself a new ma,
I don't really want her, but it's up to me da.
He said he needs a woman about the house,
So I am quiet just like a mouse.

When I close my eyes, I see your face,
And ma I am missing your warm embrace.
She will not hold me the way that you did,
I know she thinks I'm a spoilt kid.

To see you once more, my life I would give,
As days without you I don't want to live.
Why you went away I don't understand,
I just want you back to hold my hand.

Come back from heaven you've had enough rest,
If you do, I promise to be the best.
I will make sure to do what I'm told,
And it will be me you won't have to scold.

I'll make you laugh and smile every day,
All of your pain I'll chase away.
Come back to us and da won't remarry,
As it's only you that he should carry.

Angel Grace

A little angel waits on a cloud up above,

Looking down she searches for a family to love.

She hears many cries and asks can she go,

But every time she is told no.

To a certain woman you surely belong,

But you must wait until she is strong.

Her arms long to hold you but her heart isn't ready,

For she has just lost your brother Teddy.

The angel waited for many a day,

Looking down at her mammy as she did pray.

One day she was told to go wait in line,

There's no need to worry for you'll be fine.

So from a cloud the little angel flew,

In the warmth of her mother's belly she grew.

The moment her mother looked at her face,

She proudly said you're my Angel Grace.

Now I'm a mother because of you,

But I'll tell you about your brother too.

Angel looked to heaven and at god she smiled,

As she saw love through the eyes of a child.

A Special Song

I sit by his window at dawn every morning,
As I look inside, I see him yawning.
I sing good morning and how are you,
He opens his window and says the same too.

I eat the crumbs that he leaves for me,
Then I fly back to my nest in the tree.
I watch as he leaves to start his day,
He always turns and looks my way.

I was so small when I fell from my nest,
To make me better he did his best.
I could have been left alone on the ground,
Who would have known as I made no sound?

He returned me safe to my mother,
Now I see him as my big brother.
I had met a human who'd opened his heart,
And from that day we've not been apart.

I know without him I'd never have grown,
Or be here today with hatchlings of my own.
I sing for him a special song,
And thank the way he made me strong.

A Year Gone

It's been a year, where did it go?

Time it waits for no one, I know.

In my heart it hasn't been a day,

For it's there you'll always stay.

We spread your ashes and you did fly,

Like a bird up to the sky.

You became a star so bright,

Shining down on us each night.

Now there are things you'll only see,

From your home far away from me.

Each new life will make you smile,

And we'll meet again in a little while.

I know your blessings are sent from above,

To keep safe the ones you love.

You will always be around,

Though you do not make a sound.

A part of you we keep and treasure,

How much we love you nothing can measure.

Each night I know you'll shine once more,

And tonight, you'll shine brighter than ever before.

Bad News

I held the phone and heard him speak,

The news he gave made my knees go weak.

"There is no cure that we can find,

It's far too deep inside your mind".

My brains become a bomb that's ticking,

My funeral songs I now am picking.

I don't see myself as sick,

For my family I hope it's over quick.

For many years I tried to win,

Now I'm forced to just give in.

No more medicine or blood extracted,

You can imagine just how I reacted.

It wasn't for me I started to worry,

For the sake of my family I prayed death would hurry.

The aftermath they will go through,

And there is nothing that I can do.

A better place maybe I'll go,

The truth or not only time will show.

I wish to die with little regret,

As for the moment it's not over yet.

Baile Átha Cliath

In Dublin's fair city you can see the spire,
Each time I see it I think it gets higher.
People sit and beg out on the street,
Some without even shoes on their feet.

If you are looking for Dublin Zoo,
Phoenix Park is the place you go to.
There you will find wild Fallow deer,
But not to all they will appear.

Road works they leave many confused,
And all the drivers are not amused.
The GPO is still standing tall,
Despite many a bullet piercing each wall.

Trinity College and the Book of Kells,
Is one of the tours that easily sells.
The National Museum and Gallery,
Is another place that you should see.

The River Liffey flows strong and fast,
Taking with it many lives in the past.
O'Connell Bridge is crossed by so many,
As is the bridge called the Ha'penny.

Lively Temple Bar is the place to be,

Named after William and his family.

On Grafton street you'll see many a shopper,

And the odd busker who's a real showstopper.

Molly Malone stands with her cart,

All do admire this fine work of art.

In Stephen's Green on a warm day,

Some people like to jog while others stay.

On a Dublin tour bus, you're sure to see,

Many a place unknown to me.

Moore street I know and Talbot too,

And at my age those streets will do.

Through streets the Luas goes a fast pace,

Taking its passengers to many a place.

Driving the wrong way will cause you to meet,

Cars facing you on a one-way street.

The crowd and the noise are not my scene,

I much prefer silence if you know what I mean.

In the heart of the city I may not belong,

But my connection to it will always be strong.

Barber

I am a barber that cuts hair for free,

Are you brave enough to walk with me?

I go to places that hide the unknown,

Just to remind them that they're not alone.

To them I chat as they take a seat,

I've yet to see a single deadbeat.

Down on their luck is what they are,

Without a house or a flashy car.

Cutting their hair and giving them hope,

Helping them feel like they can cope.

Some try to pay but I always refuse,

Their trust in me I'd never abuse.

I have a skill that is worth sharing,

For not everyone is cruel and uncaring.

I'll do my part as long as I can,

What can you do for your fellow man?

A person is judged by what others see,

But I do not care what they think of me.

When I am done, I return home,

In my cardboard box I smile alone.

Breaking

At night I often curl up in a ball,

Banging my head off the brick wall.

A razor blade held to my skin,

To cut away the demons within.

Handfuls of hair till I'm nearly bald,

Though alopecia people think it is called.

Eating all around till I get sick,

Wishing my body thin as a stick.

Breaking all mirrors so I can't see,

The ugliness I see in me.

Trying to remove the voices in my head,

Before it's too late and I wind up dead.

To understand, you must be in my shoes,

Start with my diary as it has clues.

You look at me and think I am fine,

But I am close to crossing the line.

When I am gone please save your tears,

For you haven't cared about me in years.

I don't want pity for we both know it's fake,

Now that I have no more you can take.

Cat and Bird

Relaxing in the garden as my cat chases a bird,

I find it quite amusing, so I don't say a word.

My cat thinks it can fly and jumps off the fence,

While the bird is staring at all his nonsense.

Landing on the ground my cat is confused,

As the bird flies just above his head looking quite amused.

My cat is getting angry and has another go,

But the bird is clever and doesn't fly too low.

Sitting on the fence while the cat is on the ground,

The bird starts to sing and it's a lovely sound.

Flying in the air gently landing on my cat,

They decided to be friends and together they sat.

The bird put my cat to sleep with its beautiful song,

As they formed a friendship, they didn't find so wrong.

My cat wrapped his legs around his new-found friend,

And they lay together until the day did end.

So, it made me think of all the different races,

And how we tend to lash out at those with different faces.

If we put aside rules of each identity,

We could live together in true serenity.

Crouched

Crouched in a corner battered and bruised,

Clinging to life feeling so confused.

I begged you to stop, said please no more,

You hit me harder and at me you swore.

Your arms got tired, so I crawled off the bed,

But you started to use your feet instead.

With every kick I curled in a ball,

You kept on going as I was trapped at the wall.

You finally stopped and I let out a cry,

I prayed to god to just let me die.

My head was swelling, and my heart was breaking,

Going to sleep never to awaken.

With each bang of your fists you kissed me goodbye,

You laughed in my face as I tried not to cry.

Blinded by tears and my own blood,

Over my body at last I stood.

A warm glow around me and a shining light,

An outstretched hand and the words it's alright.

I walked straight ahead with no pain or ache,

My shell was left behind, no more could it take.

Dad

Dad I pass by where you are lying,

And when I do, I always start crying.

I find it so hard to bear,

I can't believe your lying there.

I know that you are next to me,

When I start to feel so lonely.

While learning to drive, to me you did say,

Just take good care and drive your own way.

For those behind, you do not worry,

They will pass by if in a hurry.

So, when I'm driving near or far,

You're always with me in my car.

In my rearview mirror, it's not hard to see,

Your familiar reflection smiling at me.

I have improved since them days dear dad,

And to have had your support I'll always be glad.

So, to your grave I don't need to go,

To tell you dad I miss you so.

For to me you're always here,

In my rearview mirror you'll always be near.

Emerald Isle

The Emerald Isle is where I belong,

I've listened about it in many a song.

Its history is filled with the brave,

Although some of them did misbehave.

From its top to bottom you can be assured,

The fight in the Irish cannot be cured.

Legends were born and hell was raised,

As the pride of the people are always praised.

Though famine and greed took many away,

Their sacrifice is still remembered today.

Our language replaced by the words of the crown,

Though it never managed to keep us down.

We fight when we're right and when we're wrong,

Sometimes we fight for where we belong.

Though land and sea has us divided,

Our loyalty is never misguided.

If you look back at your ancestry,

You'll be amazed at its history.

You may be related to a rebel or noble,

I'm proud to be Irish, are words spoken global.

Fading Away

I watch him as he's fading away,
For him not to suffer each day I pray.
Once he was so big and strong,
Now his life he can't prolong.

His flesh barely covers his bones,
When trying to move he always moans.
His shaking hands can't hold his cup,
Although he tries, he can't sit up.

Medicated so he feels no pain,
Causing confusion inside his brain.
Taking away all his dignity,
Not showing him any sympathy.

Watching him sleep in a cold sweat,
How long he has we don't know yet.
So hard to leave but too hard to stay,
As my second dad is fading each day.

I cannot keep my tears inside,
Though from my kids I try to hide.
Broken hearted I walk away,
As in the hospital he must stay.

False Memories

Let's go back to a memory,

That you tucked away so carefully.

Allow yourself to accept,

The pain you tried to neglect.

Now open up your pandora box,

It's time to remove all of its locks.

What you thought should be hid away,

Must come out here today.

No more a boy now you're a man,

Deal with it the way I know you can.

It never happened like you thought it did,

There is no need to keep it hid.

No reason to mourn for there was no loss,

Now out the window your pain you can toss.

The separation was just a temporary thing,

Now you must cut loose your grief from its string.

No more are you bound to what happened your brother,

Understand that he wasn't replaced by another.

It's time to embrace lost time of the past,

And accept that he is your blood at last.

Fearless

I fear spiders, mice and rats,

Snakes and bees and even bats.

Alligators, eels and sharks,

And almost every dog that barks.

But only one thing would make me leave town,

If I came face to face with IT the clown.

Just seeing a picture makes my hands shake,

The thought of a close up I just can't take.

You might have a laugh and find it funny,

To face one, I'd never get enough money.

At the mere thought my heart starts to pound,

So please do warn me if you see one around.

Acting real brave, I can do in my head,

But face to face I'd fall down dead.

Though if a clown stood between me and my child,

I'd forget my fear and become wild.

I'd be like catwoman and tear him to shreds,

If he put a finger upon one of their heads.

I am a coward and this you will see,

Until you test the mother in me.

Forgotten

Though you see me through your eyes,

I know the real me you don't recognise.

I ask you who you think I am,

And if you know who is my mam.

You say that you are trying to think,

As I start to wish I had a drink.

Was it at school you ask at last,

Completely forgetting about your past.

I ask if you remember your baby,

You reply, I'm not sure but maybe.

Do I look familiar at all?

As inside my tears start to fall.

I wasn't prepared at least not today,

It's like my mam has died and gone away.

Now I am a stranger to you,

There is nothing more I can do.

I stand alone my world torn apart,

As I watch you with a broken heart.

It wasn't meant to end this way,

I pray my children never see this day.

Goodbye

If I could make a wish come true,

I'd wish death it was pain free for you.

I sit by your bed holding your hand,

I know you hear me and understand.

You're not that old but death calls your name,

And when you're gone life won't be the same.

Such a strong man who worked hard in life,

But you started to give up when you lost your wife.

Your lungs became weak, but your heart stayed strong,

As I watch you now, I know it won't be long.

Memories of you forever I'll treasure,

To have known you was a great pleasure.

Until you go, I will stay near,

Dying alone you don't have to fear.

If it was something that I could do,

To the gates of heaven, I'd gladly take you.

You were a man so loving and kind,

Sure to live on in each heart and mind.

Tá grá agam duit, and it makes me sad,

For I'm saying goodbye to my second dad.

Grandad

To my dearest grandad now we are apart,

God did not just take you; he also took my heart.

It was very sudden the day you went away,

You were just too special for god to let you stay.

If he made you suffer then tell him from me,

It was too unfair he should have let you be.

To see your smiling face once more I will have to wait,

Until we meet again behind heavens' gate.

Now I pray for justice though it won't bring you back,

The strength to forgive so soon is something that I lack.

I just need some answers then I can close that door,

And return to the living the way I was before.

Please forgive me grandad this pain is hard to bear,

Do not think that I've grown cold and no longer care.

I do not know exactly what our god had planned,

But he must have had a reason when he took your hand.

On the day we meet again maybe I'll forgive,

But for now, I can't forget he didn't let you live.

Will you have a word with god when you're standing near,

Ask him to send some strength to the ones that you hold dear.

Grandad's Island

My grandad was a sailor with tattoos on each arm,

He had a cheeky smile and a lot of charm.

He would tell us stories about places that he went,

But he would never tell us the reasons he was sent.

He told us of an island that was filled with treasure,

And about its people that brought him so much pleasure.

He said no amount of money could ever compare,

To the beauty of the people who were living there.

He said that they would gift him each time he did leave,

As it would make him return or so they did believe.

He said he'd love to take us, but it was forbidden,

As from most of the world they remained hidden.

We believed each story for grandad never lied,

And he spoke about it right until he died.

I know that his spirit returned to that place,

For I watched a smile remain on his face.

I became a sailor when I got much older,

Each time I sailed I felt his hand upon my shoulder.

Never did I find the island of my dreams,

For exactly where it was only grandad knew it seems.

Hackers

My dearest friend your mind is dying,

I smile at you but inside I'm crying.

You speak of people I do not know,

For you had met them so long ago.

It's as if hackers have entered your mind,

And rewired your brain just to be unkind.

It was the one thing that you did fear,

Diagnosed as dementia though we all see it so clear.

The spark in your eyes starts with a flicker,

But it goes away each time a bit quicker.

You take lots of tablets to ease the pain,

As control of your mind the hackers do gain.

What is the reason for hurting one so frail?

Taking your glow and leaving you pale.

If they can hack in why can't they just hack out?

Or at least explain what it's all about.

I know one day you'll forget my name,

And your brain hackers will be to blame.

One way or the other you'll return home,

Until that day I won't leave you alone.

Hacksaw Ridge

Smoke and fire fill the air,

The smell of death, nothing can compare.

Soldiers blown up in pieces,

As the death count quickly increases.

Bullets flying day and night,

Wounded soldiers still trying to fight.

Losing limbs but not their pride,

Fighting as brothers' side by side.

One man was refusing to carry a gun,

For he didn't want to kill anyone.

Trying to break him and send him back,

They realised no courage did he lack.

He did his duty on the battlefield,

And his courage he clearly revealed.

Because of Desmond Doss and his belief,

Not allowing his faith turn to grief.

Let me get one more, to god he did say,

In the end he took 75 men away.

Hacksaw Ridge forever etched in his mind,

And all the men he had to leave behind.

Hush

Hush little girl don't say a word,

Never mind the screaming that you just heard.

Hide in your wardrobe or under your bed,

For if he finds you then he'll take your head.

Hush little girl don't you dare scream,

You better believe me that this is no dream.

Don't make a move or stand in the light,

Or this will surely be your last night.

Hush little girl don't take a breath,

Or you will surely face your death.

Stay in the shadow with your eyes closed,

Before all your insides are exposed.

Hush little girl don't try to crawl,

Or he will pin you against the wall.

He'll skin you alive and feast on your bones,

For no one around can hear your moans.

Hush little girl don't try to be brave,

Or he'll be out digging your grave.

Thrown in a sack to be forgotten,

Only discovered after you've rotten.

I Have

I have bones beneath my skin,

I have emotions running deep within.

I have voices in my head,

I have moments that I dread.

I have dreams I won't let go,

I have much to learn I know.

I have doubts about the sane,

I have fears that still remain.

I have words that go unspoken,

I have a soul that is unbroken.

I have places I want to see,

I have roots strong as a tree.

I have the will to make some changes,

I have the strength to let it take ages.

I have a vision of the future for me,

I have much love that wants to be free.

I have the heart of a warrior true,

I have a gift and so do you.

I have belief we are all the same,

I have a target and for it I'll aim.

Imaginary Friend

I sit and talk with my imaginary friend,

For upon him I can depend.

We talk about life and how it is tough,

He says carry on when I've had enough.

He gives me advice and says I should share,

My poetry with people who care.

Refusing to accept any negativity,

He tells me words are my reality.

Guiding my pen when my hand starts to shake,

Telling me that I can take a break.

Pushing me forward towards my goal,

Reminding me I have a strong soul.

Saying to me that things will be fine,

If I believe I'll see each sign.

For it was god who sent my friend,

Promising to be with me till the end.

No one can see him though he is there,

For it's with their eyes they always stare.

If with their hearts they had a look,

He'd open their minds just like a book.

IVF

Over forty years since IVF started,

Healing so many who were broken hearted.

Taking their pain and giving them joy,

To hold in their arms a girl or boy.

Is it playing god with such technology?

I believe that we owe no apology.

For every human that is created,

Should never feel that they are hated.

A little girl born to be number one,

Giving new hope to those who had none.

Yes, it has changed the world's population,

But it's a reason for great celebration.

Forever changing as we advance,

Making it possible for those with no chance.

Yes, the expense is truly draining,

But the successful will not be complaining.

Those who go through it now have a voice,

And it is them who make the choice.

This is a way that should not be taunted,

For too many babies are born unwanted.

LIFE

In each life there comes a time,

It happens without reason or rhyme.

You look around at things you know,

As part of you wants to let go.

Moving forward to be stopped in your track,

But there is no turning back.

No up or down, no left or right,

Nowhere to go try as you might.

At that moment you just stand frozen,

Is this the life that you have chosen?

Nowhere to run and nowhere to hide,

Everything lost even your pride.

Down so low and sinking fast,

No escaping from your past.

Will someone come and rescue you?

And if they don't what will you do?

Will you stand still and wait for the end?

Or will you reach out to find a friend?

One who'll be there for you day and night,

Reassuring you that things will be alright.

Lost at Sea

I sit all alone on a deserted beach,

As I look at the horizon out of my reach.

I think about walking into the sea,

And wonder would anyone really miss me.

Removing my shoes, I walk along the shore,

Life it is hard, and I can take no more.

I have no home no job or money,

There is no one to call me honey.

Standing still as my toes sink in the sand,

This really was not what I had planned.

Free as a bird I started to travel,

Not very sure when my dreams did unravel.

The ocean greets me asking to play,

So on the land I do not stay.

The water it touches each part of my skin,

As it pulls me further within.

I feel myself sinking but I do not fight,

For like a bird I will soon take flight.

The ocean it claims each part of me,

As I become another lost one at sea.

Love Letters

A tired young soldier sat down one night,

To two different women he began to write.

The first was his mother who had now become old,

The second was his young love who he longed to hold.

To his mother he wrote don't fear for your son,

I'm still your boy though I now carry a gun.

You raised me well mam and now I'm a man,

To make you proud, I'll do all I can.

To his girlfriend he wrote you're my special one,

My love for you burns bright like the sun.

I wait for the day when I'll walk through your door,

And hold you close in my arms once more.

To you I'll never use the word goodbye,

Instead I'll see you soon, love your soldier boy.

Although he had so much more to say,

He finished off and put them away.

The letters he wrote helped ease his pain,

In times when he felt like he was going insane.

Feelings of love and feelings of hate,

He did his best to separate.

He could not confess he felt scared and alone,
Or how much he wished that he was at home.
Each day he would fight for his country with pride,
Though the release of each bullet killed him inside.

Killing so many was not what he'd planned,
He couldn't explain for they wouldn't understand.
All nameless faces that stayed in his mind,
The fate of a soldier sure is unkind.

He couldn't sleep or rest his head,
He longed to go home and lie in his bed.
Tired one day he couldn't see clearly,
For on his mind were the ones he loved dearly.

A bullet was fired, and it pierced his heart,
From his loved ones forever, he now had to part.
He died with a smile upon his face,
Like he was being held in a warm embrace.

No more love letters would be received,
Reading his words together they grieved.
Each day his loved ones stand by his grave,
Missing their soldier boy who was so brave.

Mother Did You Leave Me

Mother did you leave me cos I wasn't planned?

Or did you have no one to give you a hand?

Did you let me go without seeing my face?

Or did you try to hold me tight in a warm embrace?

Mother did you leave me, so I'd be out of sight?

Or did you try to do for me what you thought was right?

Did you think leaving me behind was the best solution?

Or did your family threaten you with an institution?

Mother did you leave me cos you were forced to give me life?

Or was it because you were no one's wife?

Did you let me go to avoid going crazy?

Or have you ever thought of me and really missed your baby?

Mother did you leave me without thinking twice?

Or was it because you had no other choice?

Did you just forget and never think of me?

For it's you I search in every woman I see.

Mother did you leave me and forever say goodbye?

Or are you out there searching for me as you cry?

Will I get to see you before my life is through?

For here I am waiting to be reunited with you.

My Best Friend

Another day I must spend,

Without you my best friend.

When you left, I felt so broken,

Then you sent a special token.

You sent me a little girl,

I hold her tight and often twirl.

I know you're near when I see her smile,

And we'll meet again in a little while.

I remember each special time,

When I felt your hand in mine.

I miss you more on Mother's Day,

I wish you hadn't gone away.

You went to a better place,

Now I close my eyes to see your face.

I must go on I know it's true,

But every day I'm missing you.

Every night when I'm asleep,

For you mam I always weep.

Though from me you went away,

In my heart you'll always stay.

My Children

I look at my children and I often see,

Traces of all the good that's in me.

Each one of them are thoughtful and kind,

They never have badness in mind.

None of them look exactly the same,

My son has no brother and that's a shame.

Each one of my daughters I truly adore,

I don't believe I could love them more.

For me each one is a true beauty,

And now I've a grandson who's a real cutie.

My son is the youngest though he towers above,

Me and his sisters who he does truly love.

I know I am blessed, and I am grateful,

May they go through life never feeling hateful.

For if they have doubts or are feeling fear,

They know their mother is always near.

If I could help their dreams come true,

There isn't a thing that I wouldn't do.

The best parts of me to them I did give,

And when I'm gone, in them I'll still live.

My Choice

You try to take away my voice,

Imagining I have no choice.

Let me make this very clear,

I don't intend to disappear.

I will be heard throughout the land,

The world's attention I'll command.

You think I will get frightened away,

But I get stronger every day.

I will emerge from all the violence,

No longer will I keep my silence.

Now it's time for me to rise,

And tear away your web of lies.

You were foolish to believe,

Victory I'd never achieve.

For now you know that you were wrong,

And on this earth I do belong.

If this is a fight to the bitter end,

My beliefs I will defend.

You will not see me cower in shame,

Now I have lit my inside flame.

My Head Is My Home

I think of my home comforts now I am far away,

I remember clearly how I used to spend my day.

It wasn't on a farm where each had a chore,

Nor was it in a library with old books galore.

It wasn't down by the river trying to catch a fish,

Nor was it in the kitchen making a tasty dish.

Never did I wander about a marketplace,

Or get tired training so I could win a race.

I didn't get to climb up to a mountain top,

Or plough any field to get it ready for its crop.

I didn't milk some goats or shear any sheep,

Nor lie out with the stars so they could watch me sleep.

I lived in house as the youngest of five,

Where my love for adventure helped me stay alive.

The places I would travel by night and by day,

Are the places I visit now I am grown today.

I carry my home comforts with me in my head,

So, I can live many lives and never feel dead.

For all the things I didn't do I've done many more,

No more must I settle for the life I had before.

My Last Words

I wonder what my last words will be,

When I leave this world for eternity.

Who will be there right by my side?

And who will come to be my guide?

Will it be slow and give me time?

To say goodbye to all who are mine.

If it is fast and I go in a flash,

Please let me be alone if I crash.

How will I say goodbye to all of my babies?

Who have now become a young man and ladies.

Will I just say I'll see you all soon?

As slowly my spirit leaves the room.

Perhaps I will say yes, I forgived,

Although I couldn't while I lived.

Maybe I'll say never forget,

How much I loved until my death.

Or my last words could also be,

Thank god my spirit is gonna be free.

I can't tell for sure and I'm happy to wait,

I'm in no hurry to see heaven's gate.

Not My Year

This sure has been one hell of a year,

I am so glad that the end is near.

There were a few times I tried to fake it,

Even some doubts that I would make it.

But here I am still standing strong,

Fighting to find a place I belong.

Homelessness, poverty and heartbreak too,

Are just a few things I have gone through.

As sure as the sun rises each day,

This Phoenix will fight to have her say.

For each time I rise from the flames of doubt,

I gather strength and louder I shout.

Love me or hate me that is your choice,

It doesn't matter you won't silence my voice.

I am a woman who likes her own way,

But I'm a good friend at the end of the day.

I must admit it was not my year,

But I will not fade and disappear.

You're very welcome to tag along,

For it is friendship that makes us strong.

Now You Know

The world goes by, but you stay still,
You want to move but never will.
In your bed you must lie,
Inside your head you want to die.

How did you get to where you are?
You didn't mean to crash your car.
Only a few drinks is all you had,
But you drove cos you were mad.

She said so much you couldn't stay,
You had to leave and get away.
She got in and wouldn't leave,
Now for her you'll always grieve.

You don't know how you hit the wall,
For you can't remember it at all.
The last thing you saw it was her face,
Before sending her to another place.

Now there's no escaping from this hell,
Why didn't you just die as well?
Now as you lie and wait in shame,
You know drink driving's a fool's game.

Oceans Apart

The ocean that flows between you and me,

Is not as deep as my love for thee.

Though we are living miles apart,

There is no distance inside my heart.

Our love has bloomed despite the distance,

As our feelings have grown without resistance.

We cherish each moment we spend together,

And promise to love one another forever.

We do not fight for we've too much to say,

Starting in the morning till the end of the day.

Neither of us sleep without saying goodnight,

Just so we're sure each one is alright.

You travel to me most of the time,

Just to see me you'd spend every dime.

A part of each other we are united,

To have your love I am delighted.

No ocean too deep, no river too wide,

For our feelings flow along with the tide.

Though bad things fall around us like rain,

The sun always shines upon us again.

Read and Weep

Reading the papers is no fun today,

They never have anything good to say.

All they report are stories of gloom,

And of how soon we shall face our doom.

Articles on fraud, lies and deceit,

Trying to claim not many live on the street.

Buildings that burned, safety wasn't heeded,

For making money is all that was needed.

Suicides of great stars leaving us in shock,

Careless accidents forcing us to take stock.

Political views shoved in our faces,

While police are still solving old murder cases.

The rich and famous covering pages,

Some of them deserving to be locked up in cages.

Showbiz scandals rocking the nation,

While others are planned out of desperation.

Deaths of the ones who took life away,

And shortness of life for the ones with no say.

But just for once I'd like to read,

A story that doesn't make my heart bleed.

Scared

In the dark there is a light,

I hear a scream and get a fright.

I am pulled out of my bed,

Told to put my hands over my head.

I don't know what they're looking for,

They push me out of my bedroom door.

Down the stairs I am dragged,

All my stuff they took and bagged.

A gun is held up to my face,

Are they in the right place?

They scream a name I do not know,

I pray that they would just go.

There is a bang, a gunshot,

My blood runs out and it feels hot.

I fall to the floor and cannot move,

Do they have something to prove?

What was the reason for this attack?

They run away and all goes black.

I faintly hear another scream

Just then I wake up from my dream.

Stardust

What started out as a night of fun,

Turned into a tragic one.

Doors were locked with no escaping,

As young lives a fire began taking.

Screams were heard from miles around,

A sickening sight is what rescuers found.

Lives were lost and others were changed,

A cover up was quickly arranged.

214 injured and 48 dead,

How can the guilty sleep in their bed?

A man-made disaster for reasons unclear,

The truth of it all we need to hear.

No justice will ever reverse that night,

Or erase the memories of such a sight.

Affecting more than just those inside,

Their human rights should not be denied.

Turned into dust they are now stars,

For they were trapped behind doors and bars.

I know the pain will never leave,

For in Irish justice it's hard to believe.

Stirred Emotions

I come outside from inside me,

As my words become so free.

I stay a while to say hello,

And back inside each time I go.

I stir my emotions from inside my pot,

And slowly release them when they are hot.

Sometimes they boil over, but I refuse to hide,

I guess you can say it's my Irish pride.

I am not sorry for the words that I write,

And if you disapprove don't get uptight.

Nothing can stop the words in my head,

As they are often easily lead.

With my head and heart, I'll stir each day,

For you can be sure I'll have my say.

It may be vocal or even lyrical,

Positive or even cynical.

Either way I will be real,

And reveal exactly how I feel.

In each poem you're sure to see,

Many different sides of me.

Switched

Two little girls were mixed up at birth,

To be raised each ends of the earth.

One grew up healthy and strong,

The other was sick all day long.

With not long left for their girl to survive,

Shocking news to her parents did arrive.

This little girl that you call your own,

Does not belong in your hearts or your home.

There was a mix up on the day she was born,

For on two girls a name tag was not worn.

A student nurse didn't know what to do,

So she gave the wrong baby to you.

As they sat by their girl's bedside,

For the loss of two daughters the silently cried.

They cried for the daughter they had never met,

And for the one taking her last breath.

They lovingly took her body home,

For in their hearts she was their own.

The bond of blood maybe it's strong,

But how much your loved shows where you belong.

Taken Away

They took away your life today,

In fear of what you had to say.

Words don't hurt, now that's not true,

For we saw what they did to you.

Cowardly they surrounded a boy,

To do more than make you cry.

Did you get a chance to fight?

Or were they too quick in the dark of night?

Before they went and left you alone,

They made sure to take your phone.

Those who stood by and silently stared,

Please speak up and show that you cared.

Left to pick up the lives they shattered,

We will get justice for your life mattered.

May they forever see your brave face,

And be named for their disgrace.

No sentence will bring us joy,

For it can't replace our precious boy.

Your future they have taken away,

In this hell on earth we must stay.

The Future Generation

Children of today,

Are leading the way.

For a new tomorrow,

As time we all borrow.

Technology is growing,

As ideas are flowing.

Medical advances,

Giving life more chances.

Transportation is expanding,

Faster routes they are demanding.

Modern warfare is dictated,

By leaders who are hated.

Intelligence manipulated,

As objections are sedated.

Religions causing destruction,

Bombs made in mass production.

Fiction into reality,

As changes become normality.

Ruled by the future generation,

What will be our destination?

The Home I Left Behind

I was very young when I moved away,

But I still recall it to this very day.

The kettle on the boil in case someone did call,

As pictures of smiling faces hung upon the wall.

The toilet in the yard that was always cold,

And it never changed till this day I am told.

The clothes we had to hand wash and try to untangle,

So it would be easier when using the mangle.

The fire that would warm us from morning till night,

As candles did burn when we needed extra light.

The pot that always fed a dozen or more,

And quickly it would fill just like it did before.

The blankets and the duffle coats to keep us warm at night,

More than two in a bed as we would cuddle tight.

The radio that played songs we used to sing,

The daily chores that we completed each time it was spring.

Clothes that were passed down to one child or another,

That were then passed on to others by our mother.

The teardrops that fell still fresh in my mind,

When I walked away from the house I left behind.

The Old Man

An old man was told that he was dying,

He shed no tears though inside he was crying.

He thought of his children and felt such regret,

For he had some he had never met.

Living his life, he was never aware,

For all the time he just didn't care.

With the one woman he just couldn't stay,

Often it was only for a day.

Now all alone he had nowhere to go,

With no one to hold him as his tears did flow.

He was a rich man, but his wealth was no use,

His body was worn out from years of abuse.

He'd been too busy having lots of fun,

There was no time to care for anyone.

To change his past now it was too late,

For soon he'd be standing outside of Hell's gate.

Now he has learned life doesn't last,

And we can't change the mistakes of our past.

So, if we don't live and learn while alive,

Our memory will never survive.

Time Goes By

Time goes by and before we know,

We watch as our loved ones must go.

Some leave in peace while others do in pain,

As death takes away and only memories remain.

No matter how long you get to prepare,

We are never ready to no longer care.

With no explanation as to why they must leave,

Questioning god as we constantly grieve.

Nothing stands still for time moves along,

Expecting us all to become strong.

But in this world, that's cruel and unkind,

Death can cause us to lose our mind.

With so many questions we can't understand,

Why life and death are already planned.

We'll all meet again or so they say,

As we are left to wait for our last day.

We cling to the hope that all is true,

But if it isn't what can we do.

Once we are gone there's no returning,

As a place by god's side each day we are earning.

Traveller

Today I travelled through time and space,

Back to a long-forgotten place.

To a time I couldn't see,

How to be the real me.

Unafraid I held the hand,

Of my old self and I took command.

I said you can follow me,

I've found a way you can be free.

A leap of faith we took once more,

Staying together unlike before.

For part of me was left behind,

Deep inside my tired mind.

Trapped by words that were unspoken,

Until the dragon in me was awoken.

Now what held me has burned to ashes,

Unable to return in blinding flashes.

Now old and new walk hand in hand,

And united together we stand.

No more to wander torn apart,

A lost soul and a broken heart.

<u>Up</u>

Wake up,

Shake up.

Make up,

Take up.

Rise up,

Size up.

Look up,

Hook up.

Rip up,

Whip up.

Hike up,

Bike up.

Lick up,

Pick up.

Check-up,

But never feck up.

You Can't Tell Me

How to walk,

How to talk.

How to think,

How to blink.

How to dress,

How to caress.

How to react,

How to contract.

How to kiss,

How to miss.

How to command,

How to expand.

How to collect,

How to reflect.

How to own,

How to clone.

How to give,

How to live.

How to thrive,

How to survive.

Printed in Poland
by Amazon Fulfillment
Poland Sp. z o.o., Wrocław

49281994R00034